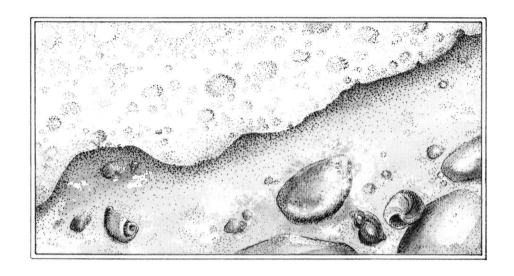

Journey OF
THE Sea Glass

illustrated by Nicole Fazio

Down East Books

This book originated from a concept by Ari Meil

ISBN 978-1-60893-177-4

Design by Lynda Chilton

Printed in China

Down East Books
www.nbnbooks.com
Distributed by
National Book Network
800-462-6420

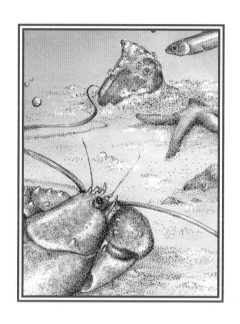

For my family, for a

lifetime of encouragement;

and for Dave, for his

everlasting patience.

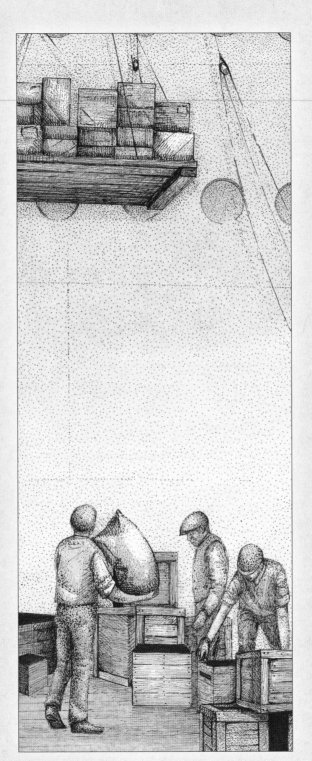

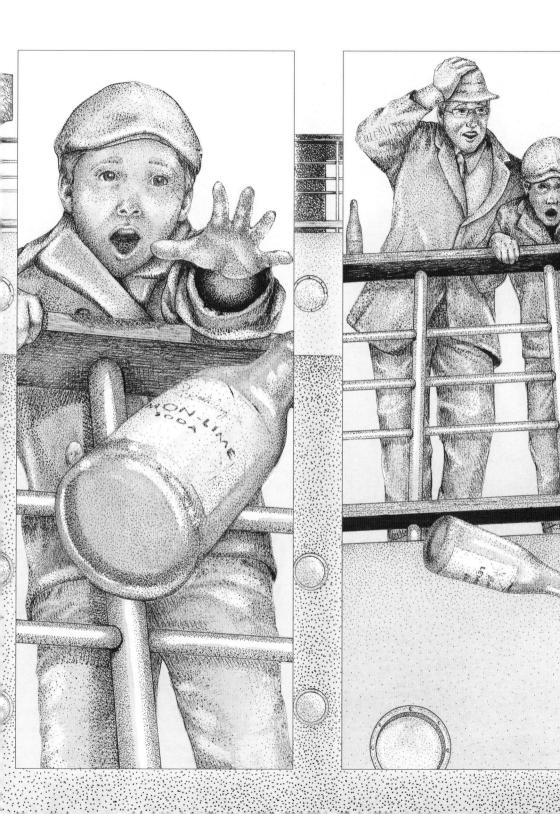

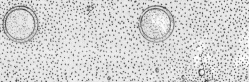

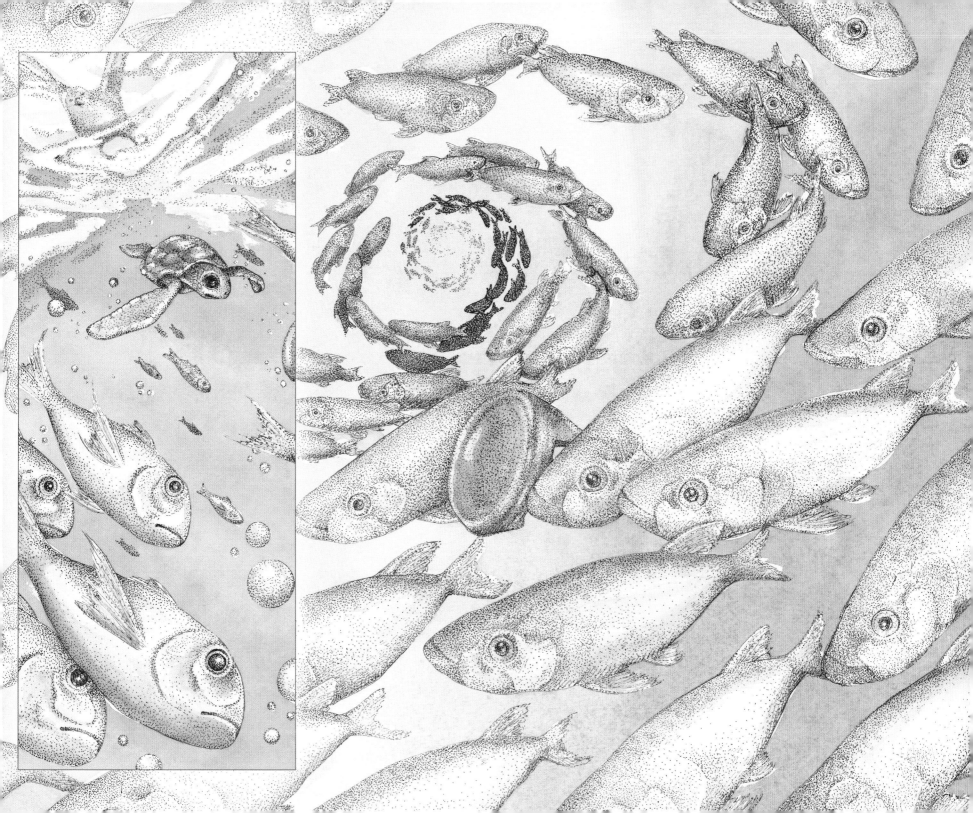

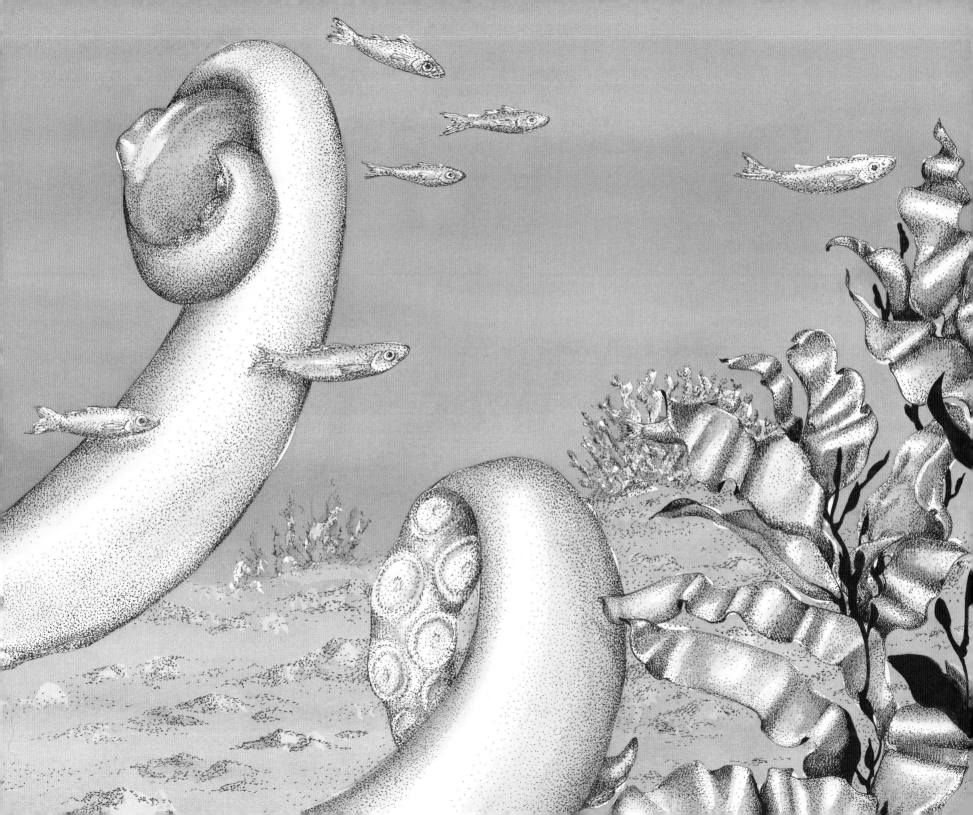